I've Broken MY BUM!

WARNING: Don't try this at home!

Dawn McMillan

Illustrated by
Ross Kinnaird

SCHOLASTIC

I've crashed my bike. I've sat with a splat!
I've broken my bum! My bum has gone flat!

I need to fix it, not a minute to waste.
I'm heading home in hurry and haste.

Calamity! Catastrophe!

A terrible blow.
My bum bits fall on the floor below.

A disaster, it's true. What can I do?
I have an idea. I'll get some glue.

I see a tray up there, on the shelf.
A tray to work on while I fix myself.

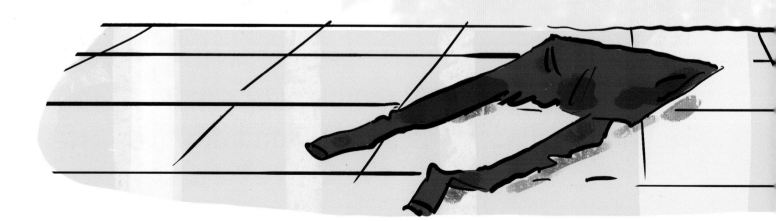

I find all the bum pieces from under the sink.
I glue them together, pink shapes to pink.

Round bits to round bits.
Flat bits to fit.
And ...

Victory! Triumph!

My bum is intact.

I don't mind at all that it still has a crack!

With the pieces together my bum looks like new.
But to put my bum back I need HEAPS of glue!

I'm steady. I'm ready. I press my bum on.
I look in the mirror and …
Something is wrong!

There's a terrible problem! A problem that's new.
My bum is glued on, but the tray is glued too.

I twist and I pull. I tug with my might.

I wriggle. I jiggle. But the glue's holding tight.

I think, a bum with a tray is not a good sight.

Seems I'm destined to have a bum with a tray.
But how can I dress, shaped in this way?

Ah, I have an idea. I see it's quite clear.
I need to snip my pants back here at the rear.

Cut out the back to let the tray through.
A fantastic solution, and easy to do.

But ...

Our mother is looking! Does she want a son
with a tray shape stuck on the back of his bum?

No. She wants to fix it, to give it a trim.
Dad has an idea, but I'm not keen for him ...
to do anything!

Because my new bum is ...

Perfect for sliding in mud or in snow.
I've a built-in sledge, **ready to go!**

Great for sand dunes! I have a blast!
I eat lots of beans to make me go fast!

Perfect for winning
at paintball, you see.

And surfing big waves,
no wipeouts for me!

Hill-sliding too – I didn't see ...

Being attached to a tray is TOTALLY fine!
See, all my friends want a bum like mine!

But now ...

I'm going out for dinner.
I need to look like a winner.
I'll dress in my best
with my bright yellow vest.

The dress code? Don't worry, I'll 'crack it'.
I'll wear my purple-and-green spotted jacket.

But ...

This jacket's not right.

This jacket's too tight!

It's not a good fit – a jacket and tray!

What can I do? What can I say?

And then I know exactly what to say ...

I say ...
Jackets away!

Let's go and play!

About the author

Dawn McMillan lives in Waiomu, a small coastal village on the western side of the Coromandel Peninsula in New Zealand. She lives with her husband, Derek, and their cat, Lola. She writes in her little backyard studio – some serious books and lots of silly books, like this one, another bum story.

About the illustrator

Ross Kinnaird is an illustrator and graphic designer. He lives in Auckland. When he's not illustrating a book, or being cross with his computer, he enjoys most activities to do with the sea. He loves visiting schools to talk about books and drawing and has been known to draw really funny cartoons of teachers!

First published in 2019 by Oratia Media
This edition published in the UK in 2020 by Scholastic Children's Books
Euston House, 24 Eversholt Street
London NW1 1DB, UK
A division of Scholastic Ltd
www.scholastic.co.uk
London ~ New York ~ Toronto ~ Sydney ~ Auckland
Mexico City ~ New Delhi ~ Hong Kong

Text copyright © Dawn McMillan 2019
Illustrations copyright © Ross Kinnaird 2019
ISBN 978 0 7023 0002 8